MW00946012

Lily, the snail who wanted to go Fast

(and other Life Lesson Limericks)

CHRISTOPHER MILLER

To order additional copies of this book, contact:
Xlibris
844-714-8691
www.Xlibris.com
Orders@Xlibris.com

ISBN: Softcover   978-1-6641-3553-6
         Hardcover   978-1-6641-3555-0
         EBook   978-1-6641-3554-3

Library of Congress Control Number: 2020920036

Print information available on the last page

Rev. date: 10/08/2020

To my dear momma Mary Margaret Miller who gave me the love of books and reading. I spent many car trips as a boy sitting on her lap reading all the billboards to her. Sadly dementia will prevent her from enjoying this book because I think she would love it.

Lily, the Snail Who Wanted to Go Fast
(and other Life Lesson Limericks)

Eric the chubby aardvark really loved to eat ants.

But he ate so many that the other aardvarks made fun
of him because he couldn't buckle his pants.

But when the cold winter came and the aardvarks had to cuddle,

To keep warm they all wanted chubby Eric in the middle of their huddle.

So NEVER judge another based on first glance.

Chi Chi the Chinchilla loved to kick the soccer ball.

She hoped to make the team but they said she was too small.

But Chi Chi was determined so she practiced day and night.

She practiced all her ball skills with her left and with her right.

Chi Chi not only made the team but was the best player of them all.

Paige was a penguin who really loved to sing.

But living in Antarctica was not her favorite thing.

So she practiced her singing till she was good
enough to make money with her mouth.

She became so successful she was able to move to the sunny South!

All of Paige's hard work paid off so she could live like a king.

Dennis the Dolphin was loved by Meg the Manatee.

Meg's family said, "He's not like us, can't you see?"

But Meg knew Dennis had a kind heart and did become his wife.

And because they loved each other they had a wonderful life.

They showed all of their friends that happiness was the key.

Tina the Tiny Tuna was the smallest fish in her school.

All the big tunas laughed at Tina and made her feel like a fool.

One day all the big fish got caught in the fishermen's net.

But Tina was able to free them because she was
too tiny for the fishermen to get.

From that day forward Tina the Tiny Tuna did rule!

Pete and Paul Plecostomus lived at the bottom of the sea.

Pete was always working while Paul was quite lazy.

When pretty Penelope one day swam by,

It was hardworking Pete who caught her eye.

Pete and Penelope swam off happy together while Paul was left quite lonely.

Aaron the Albatross was sad because he was the dirtiest bird.

Insults and ridicule are all he ever heard.

But when the hunter came looking for his prey,

Aaron's dirty feathers were like camouflage and helped the colony get away.

Never again did Aaron the Albatross hear a discouraging word.

Katie the Koala didn't like the taste of eucalyptus.

The other Koalas made her cry and said, "That's weird, you can't be one of us."

But after they had eaten too much and couldn't stay awake,

Up the tree came a very large and very hungry snake.

But our alert hero Katie saved the day, scaring off
the snake by making a loud ruckus!

Albert was an old miniature horse.

He lived next to a miniature golf course.

He loved to play but his friends said, "Give it up, you old fogie."

But Albert practiced and practiced until he almost never shot a bogie.

Albert became the first miniature horse putt putt force.

Ralphie the Rhinoceros was born with a purple horn.

Because of this, poor Ralphie felt the other rhinos' scorn.

But when it came time for the young rhinos to choose their wives,

It was Ralphie with whom the rhino cows wanted to spend the rest of their lives.

For that purple horn made Ralphie the most handsome rhino ever born.

Amy the Earthworm was afraid to get dirty.

A dangerous predicament for a worm certainly.

But Mom and Dad taught Amy that she had to face her fear.

So she got going bravely and learned to dig deep in high gear.

And Amy the Earthworm never had to worry about the early birdy.

Diana was a duckling who hated wearing glasses.

At school, she was called Four Eyes in all of her classes.

But Momma always told her not to worry about her looks.

Momma taught her to concentrate on bettering herself and always hit the books.

And thanks to that advice all of her classmates Diana surpasses.

Abby the Alligator liked to be left alone.

She hated everybody always contacting her on her phone.

One day she lost her temper and her cellphone she did eat.

Now her belly lights up every time someone calls, texts, or tweets.

Abby learned when she gets mad it's best to just let out a little moan.

Eleanor the Elephant had a peanut allergy.

This made her very sad for they were her favorite food, you see.

But her mommy took good care of her and fed her very well.

She loved pancakes and spaghetti and oysters on the half shell.

Eleanor learned to take what life gave her and was happy as could be.

Lily was a snail who dreamed of going fast.

She hated the fact she was always getting passed.

Lily hated moving so slow and always being late.

So bound and determined she learned to roller-skate.

And now Lily the snail never gets there last.

CPSIA information can be obtained
at www.ICGtesting.com
Printed in the USA
BVHW020320181120
593596BV00002B/3